Ticket to Faerie

For ten years, Alyssa's grandmother sent her magical gifts that didn't work. But, when Alyssa correctly, for once, follows the instructions that came with her 16th birthday present, she finds herself in Faerie, desperately trying to bring home a way to save her grandmother's life.

Ticket to Faerie

Alyssa searches Faerie for a way to save her grandmother's life, but stumbles into an adventure that endangers her own.

F.I. Goldhaber

As a reporter, editor, business writer, and marketing communications consultant, F.I. Goldhaber produced news stories, feature articles, essays, editorial columns, and reviews for newspapers, corporations, governments, and non-profits in five states. Now, her poems, short stories, novelettes, essays, and reviews appear in paper, electronic, and audio magazines, ezines, newspapers, calendars, and anthologies. She published seven erotic novels and novellas under another name.

In addition, F.I. shares her words at events in Portland, Seattle, Salem, Keizer and on the radio. She appeared at venues such as Wordstock, Oregon Literary Review, PDX SynesthiA, bookstores, libraries, and community colleges; gives presentations on subjects as diverse as marketing, writing erotica, and building volunteer organizations; and taught Introduction to Indie Publishing at Portland Community College and as a weekend intensive.

http://goldhaber.net/

Ticket to Faerie

Fantastic Worlds Publishing

ISBN: 978-1-937839-11-6

Copyright © 2014 by F.I. Goldhaber
Cover design by Joel Goldhaber
Copyright © 2014 by F.I. Goldhaber

Fantastic Worlds Publishing
http://fantasticworldspublishing.com
P.O. Box 80766
Portland OR 97280

Originally published electronically by
Uncial Press
an imprint of GCT, Inc.

Acknowledgements

Many thanks to all those I have learned from through the years, especially the Wordos professional writers workshop and Larry Brooks. Thanks also to those who have freely shared their knowledge online notably Dean Wesley Smith and Kristine Kathryn Rusch. Those who inspired me to pursue writing from an early age include Ruth Wright my fifth and sixth grade teacher at Randolph Elementary School in Huntsville, Alabama, Nancy Travis my freshman English teacher at Clear Creek High School in Texas, and most prominently my parents, Jerry and Bev Goldhaber. Very special thanks to my editor, Laurie Lawhon of Fine Tune Your Words, Dr. Tanya Goldhaber for her assistance with this story, and my beloved husband Joel Goldhaber.

Ticket to Faerie

Alyssa slapped the thick envelope against the palm of her hand. She recognized the fancy script from the flat nib of Grandma's fountain pen. Every year she received a similar packet within a few days of her August birthday. Nanna, Mom's mother, sent checks on Alyssa's birthday and at Christmas that she could spend on clothing or music. But her father's mother only sent junk.

When she was a child, Alyssa pretended that Grandma's magical charms would work and attempted to follow the detailed and silly instructions. They never did whatever Grandma promised, but Alyssa had fun pretending. Of course, she used to read fairy tales, too. Now, as she entered her sixteenth year, she wanted more than pretend magic. Nanna had sent a sizeable check in honor of the milestone. Even though her mom would only let her spend half of it, Alyssa had enough for six albums and a pair of new skate shoes.

With a snort, she loosened the envelope flap with her thumb, and pulled out a piece of white parchment paper covered with neat black script.

Dearest Alyssa,

I know you've found my gifts disap-pointing in the past. The only reason the magic never worked for you is because you refuse to follow my instructions pre-cisely. I've chosen a very special gift for your sixteenth birthday and I hope you've finally matured enough to take advantage of it. You're only permitted three visits in a lifetime, dear. Please make the most of this one.

Love,
Grandma

Alyssa used her fore and middle fingers to scissor the envelope open wide enough so she could peer inside to see what else it contained. She withdrew the square document, not sure if the material was thick cardstock or thin PVC. The words "Magical Carnet" were written in bold letters across the top of one side. The rest of the script crowded together in letters so small, she had to squint to read.

"Good for one round trip to any destination within the Kingdoms of Faerie that the bearer chooses. Must use within one year of receipt. Must return within one month of departure. To use ticket, bearer must arrive at the station a half hour before scheduled departure. Reservations recommended, but not required." On the back, at the top it said, "Directions:" followed by intricate descriptions of more silly requirements such as hopping on one foot and running around widdershins.

Alyssa muttered under her breath and stuffed the letter and the "ticket" back in the envelope.

"Whatcha got there, Short Stuff?" At six-foot-three, her father towered over his diminutive wife, and Alyssa had inherited her mother's height, not his.

She held up the envelope and made no attempt to keep the disappointment from her face.

"I'm sorry, Babe." Her dad leaned down and ruffled her short reddish-blond hair. "I know Mom's a few sandwiches short of a picnic, but she does love you."

"Yeah, right," Alyssa whispered. She stuck out her lower lip.

"What say we go see Mom this weekend? I'm sure she'd like that, and maybe she'll have a real present for you at her house." His grin made his freckled face, still topped with a thick mop of carrot-red hair, even more boyish. Alyssa could almost forget he was her dad and not the big brother she'd always wanted.

She wandered up to her room and tossed the envelope on top of the painted white dresser with fading fairy decals. Later, she would drag the box from the top shelf of the closet and add the envelope to all of Grandma's other gifts that her mom had insisted she keep over the years: the plastic pony that never turned into the real thing; the stuffed mermaid that only got wet when Alyssa, unable to find a swimming hole, threw it in the pool; the cream that didn't make all her freckles disappear when she turned twelve; the miniature saxophone that never improved her skills enough for her to make the jazz band and travel to D.C.

At least those gifts included something she could play with. Alyssa pulled the ticket from the envelope. *So pathetic.* She really had gotten too old to amuse herself with dolls and trinkets, never mind pretend trips to Faerie.

Mom knocked on the half-open door and let herself in. "What did your grandmother send you this year?" Although the same height, her mom looked as delicate as lace, while Alyssa felt as clunky as cotton flannel. Her mom had curves and tiny wrists and ankles. Although Alyssa hadn't inherited her father's height, he had cursed her with his stocky build. She had the same measurement for hips, chest, and waist.

Her dad had to punch an extra hole in her watch band so she could buckle it around her wrist.

Alyssa handed her mother the ticket.

She read it, smiled, and sat on the bed. "Sweetheart, have you ever wondered why you're an only child?"

Alyssa shrugged her shoulders. When she realized at the age of five that a big brother would not be forthcoming, she had begged her parents, to no avail, for a little sister.

"When your dad and I got married, we wanted children, but the doctors said I couldn't." Her mom ran her fingers through her long, almost white-blond hair. "When he was younger, your father got into some trouble and no one would approve us for adoption. Your grandmother offered to help, but she said that kind of magic would only work once. Of course, your father gave her no credence. Still, she promised me that if I followed her instructions *precisely*, I could get pregnant. Some of the things she required me to do seemed bizarre. And I had the devil of a time getting your father to cooperate on the timing. But..." Mom reached out and stroked Alyssa's cheek. Tears shimmered in her blue eyes.

"I'm sorry I never told you before, but your father was so adamant about not letting you believe in magic." Her mom stood and smoothed non-existent wrinkles out of her skirt. "You realize, don't you, that this is probably your grandmother's last gift to you?"

Alyssa nodded. The past year, grandma had spent more time in the hospital than she had at home.

"You've got a couple of weeks before school starts. You should make the trip so you can tell Grandma about your adventures." Mom left the room and closed the door.

Alyssa just stared at the dark wood, not believing Mom could put any faith in Grandma's balderdash, to use one of Dad's words. She dragged the chair from her desk over to the closet, tugged the box down from the top shelf, and went through each letter she'd received since the first one on her sixth birthday. Something always prevented her from following the instructions exactly as written, she realized. Either she hadn't understood a word, or she'd tried substituting one thing for another, figuring it wouldn't make any difference.

Alyssa thought about what Mom had told her: that she existed only because of Grandma's magic. She read the instructions on the ticket again, logged onto the Internet, and looked up widdershins. If she did everything precisely as directed and nothing happened, Mom would have to give up the notion that Grandma's magic worked. If Alyssa somehow ended up in Faerie...

Mom tapped on the door again. "Here." She handed Alyssa a black pen with a metal dragon wrapped around the shaft. "I've kept this since I used it as part of the conception spell. I searched every secondhand store and tobacco shop in Portland for it." She laughed. "Probably could find one now on the Internet, but that wasn't an option back then."

"Tobacco shop?"

"Yes." Her mother pressed the pocket clip. A blue-green flame spurted from the top of the pen and the dragon's ruby-red eyes lit up. "I don't think it has any magic beyond the one spell, but the lighter and pen still work and I thought you might like to take it with you." She left Alyssa standing with the pen in her hand and her mouth open.

After studying the copper dragon for a few minutes, Alyssa dumped her black backpack out on the bed. She hesitated, wondering what to pack for a trip to Faerie. She replaced the books and notebooks with a change of underwear, a pair of blue jeans, socks, and a t-shirt. After some thought, she added her MP3 player, cell phone, red Converse sneakers, black hoodie, energy bars, Swiss army knife, compass, flashlight, and the dragon pen.

She looked at herself in the mirror on the back of her closet door, considering her short denim skirt with a tight red tank top and yellow and green flip flops. *What does one wear to Faerie?* She blew upwards, ruffling her bangs. Wouldn't matter what she wore. *I don't look good in any of my clothes.* After slinging a strap of the backpack over her shoulder, she grabbed the black and white trucker hat that hung from a bedpost, and stuck the ticket into her skirt pocket. In the kitchen, she added several liters of bottled water to her backpack.

She found Mom sitting on the back porch. "Okay, I'm gonna try."

Her German Shepard, Max, came bounding up, excited at the prospect of going for a walk.

"You should take Max with you for protection. And, be careful, sweetie. Don't stay too long." Mom stood and wrapped her arms around Alyssa.

She hugged Mom back, found Max's leash and clipped it to his collar. "What will you tell Dad?"

"Don't worry about your father, dear." Her eyes twinkled. "I'll take care of him. Have fun."

With Max tugging at the leash, Alyssa let herself out the gate and walked down the gravel road through the surrounding woods toward the deserted school bus stop. *Like this is going to work. Not.* She adjusted her hat with the brim to the side. *Oh, well. I'll go through the motions. Maybe I'll pretend to go to Faerie. I can hide out at Tory's for a couple of days, make up some story to entertain Grandma and get Mom off my back.*

She pulled out the ticket and read the instructions again--no mention of dogs. Just before she reached the tiny wooden shelter that kept her and the neighbor kids dry in the drizzly Oregon winters, she tied Max's leash to a tree branch. "Stay, boy."

With the ticket in her left hand she walked around the empty shelter, snickering. She circled it five times widdershins, always keeping her left foot in front of her right. Then she faced the open side of the shelter and said in her best imitation of an English accent, "I say, madame, when does the next coach for Faerie leave, if you please? I was hoping to use this ticket today." She rolled her eyes, but jumped up and down on her left foot five times, careful to avoid touching the ground with her right. With her eyes closed, she turned around once. She put the ticket in her teeth, leaned down, grabbed her ankles with her hands, and stayed there until she had counted from one hundred backwards to thirty-two. *Good thing it doesn't say anything about doing this with a straight face. At least no one can see me.*

When she stood up and opened her eyes, she saw a ticket booth with a chalkboard above and a little, green-skinned woman inside. *Whoa.* She looked around the sides of the shelter/ticket booth trying to figure out how someone had rigged the illusion. *This can't be real.*

"Cancha read, girlie?" The woman pointed upward. Her black eyes looked like legless beetles and a snake wrapped around her head restrained her long green hair.

Alyssa shook her head and read the green letters. *Next coach: quarter 'til.* "Quarter 'til what?"

"Are you daft, dearie?" The woman looked at

a salamander that had wrapped itself around her wrist with its tail in its mouth. "Look, it's quarter past now. Coach'll be here in another half."

Alyssa showed her the ticket. "Can I use this?"

"Nope." The woman snatched the ticket from Alyssa and handed it to the snake. It bit the ticket and punched two holes in one end. "This's just a voucher. Where ya wanna go?"

Alyssa blinked several times, and shrugged her shoulders.

"Faerie's a big place, dearie. Ya gotta have some idea where ya wanna go, or who ya wanna meet, or what ya wanna bring back."

"Bring back." Alyssa thought of all the unkind things she'd said about Grandma, under her breath and to her friends, and the visits to the hospital she'd made excuses to avoid. Then too, if Grandma couldn't return to Faerie because she'd already visited three times, and Alyssa brought back something to help her, surely her dad would finally let her get her belly button pierced. Of course, she'd have to convince him the magic worked. Maybe her mom would help her with that.

She put her hands on the counter in front of the woman. "Could I bring back something to save my grandma?"

"'Pends. What's her problem?"

"She has cancer, pancreatic cancer."

The woman scratched at her chin. "Don't

know. I'd try Giserella's." She reached behind her, retrieved a white mouse which she handed to Alyssa. "Here's your ticket."

Alyssa cupped her hands around the little creature, but it made no move to escape. "Can I bring my dog?"

"Does your dog want to go?"

"What?"

"Does your dog want to go?" The woman leaned out the window of the ticket booth. "Hey, Max, you wanna go with this girl?"

"Yeah, her mom expects me to watch out for her."

Alyssa stared at him. Grandma had given her Max when he was just a wiggling nine-pound puppy, but she had never heard him speak before. She dropped onto the bench that protruded from one side of the ticket booth. "Don't worry, love," the mouse in her hands squeaked. "You'll get used to it."

She had to grit her teeth to avoid dropping the mouse. "I suppose all the animals in Faerie talk?"

"Just the intelligent ones."

Max laughed, or at least that's what Alyssa thought he meant by a half-howl, half-bark.

To her relief, no one spoke again until Alyssa heard horses galloping, a carriage creaking, and someone shouting. She ran to untie Max's leash. Only then did she notice that the asphalt highway that led into Hillsboro had turned into a dirt road. A team of four big bay mares pulled a purple coach almost as big as her Dad's pickup around the bend. The brawny fellow on the high front seat held the reins in big furry paws. He wore leather knee-length breeches and a homespun singlet under a leather vest. His head, on which he wore a felt woodsman's hat, resembled a grizzly bear's.

The bear jumped down from his seat and opened the coach door. "Ticket?"

Alyssa opened the hand with the mouse in it. "Good morrow, Coachman," the little creature said.

The bear tipped his hat. "Good morrow, yourself, Miss Lilse. Headed back, are we?"

"First chance I've had." The mouse crawled up Alyssa's arm, her little feet tickling Alyssa's skin, and settled on her shoulder.

The bear offered one paw to Alyssa. She used it to pull herself up into the coach. The front facing seat was occupied, so she sat on the backward one. Figures. I'll probably get sick from riding the wrong way. The bear leaned over, waited while Max jumped onto his back and from there leapt to the top of the carriage, and slammed the door. Moments later the coach lurched forward.

When her eyes adjusted to the dim light, Alyssa looked at the passengers who sat across from her on the tufted leather seat. A young woman wearing voluminous velvet skirts and a tight bodice that pressed her breasts into mounds under her chin sat next to a fox in a three-piece black gabardine suit with a matching top hat.

Alyssa closed her eyes and settled her pack next to her on the seat. Fortunately, neither the woman nor the fox offered to introduce themselves. She couldn't wrap her brain around talking mice and green-skinned ticket takers, never mind a fox dressed up as a noble.

She had no idea how long or in what direction the coach traveled, but when it stopped again, her rear felt sore and her back ached from trying to maintain her seat.

"Giserella's," the bear said.

The young woman gasped and looked at Alyssa with eyes opened wide. The fox tucked her hand under its foreleg and she leaned against him.

Alyssa swallowed hard and clutched at her pack, but let the bear help her down from the carriage. Max had already jumped down from the top of the coach and he sat on the side of the road, his leash in his mouth.

When she took the handle from him, he asked: "Can we dispense with that here? I'll keep the collar on if you insist, but," he looked from side to side, "I do have my dignity."

"Whatever," Alyssa muttered. She guessed a talking dog didn't need a leash so she tucked it into her backpack, slipped her arms into the pack's straps, and eased them up onto her shoulders. The mouse resettled on top of the strap, and Alyssa turned her head to look at it. "Do you know where we're supposed to go?"

Max raised one paw and pointed toward a path off the main road that led into a thick strand of trees. "Giserella's is that way."

Alyssa stared at Max. "How in the world do you know?" On the other side of the road, shoulder-high rows of corn lined a field behind a low stone wall. Except for the red, green, orange, blue, and pink tassels, Alyssa could be standing on a road anywhere in the western Oregon countryside. *This just can't be real.*

"Everyone knows how to get to Giserella's, love," the mouse whispered into Alyssa's ear. "The trick is to find your way out again."

Alyssa reached into the side pocket of her pack and pulled out the compass. She held it in her hand until the needle stopped moving and pointed in the direction of the path.

"Sorry, love, that's not going to do you much good here." The mouse snorted. "But then, that's why you have a ticket."

"Why not? That must be north." Alyssa pointed in the direction that the compass did.

"Turn around three times."

Alyssa blew out her breath and did as the mouse instructed. The compass needle now pointed down the road in the direction they had come. *Well, this sucks.* She put it back into her pack, wondering how many of the other items she had chosen to bring with would also prove useless. Max pranced down the trail and she followed him. After walking through the silent woods for what seemed like miles and drinking half the water in one of her bottles, she spotted a cottage nestled among the trees near the path. Smoke drifted from the brick chimney and black and purple flowers bloomed in planters hanging from the windows on either side of the purple wooden door.

Max turned off the path to follow flat stones that led to the cottage door.

Alyssa trailed after him and banged on the door.

A little girl opened it. "Yes?" She had blond pigtails, almost as long as she stood tall, and wore a purple and black checked pinafore over a starched taffeta dress with puffed sleeves and a full skirt. The dress fabric shifted between purple and black.

"We're looking for Giserella," Alyssa said.

"I'm Giserella. Why?"

"The ticket lady said I could get a magic potion from you to cure my grandma from pancreatic cancer." *She didn't say you were just a brat.*

Giserella put her little fists on her hips. "And why would I want to give you that?"

"We've got cool stuff to give you," Max said.

Alyssa glared at him.

"Oh." Giserella tilted her head to one side. "Like what?"

Max pushed his nose at the pack. The mouse stepped away from the strap and Alyssa lifted it

15

off her shoulders. She reached into the outside pocket, pulled out the compass and offered it to Giserella.

"What do I want with this?" She handed it back to Alyssa. "It won't work here."

Alyssa rummaged around in her pack, trying to decide what she could part with. Max nudged her elbow when she touched the MP3 player. Reluctantly, she withdrew it. "What about this?"

"That's more like it." The girl's lips curled upward and Alyssa noticed that her teeth came to sharp points. "Of course, this might get you a cure for breast cancer or maybe lung cancer. But, pancreatic cancer, that's a little trickier." She held the MP3 player up to her ear and shook it.

Alyssa, while trying to find the cell phone that seemed to have gotten buried in the bottom of the pack, pulled out her t-shirt and set it on the porch.

Giserella picked it up. "Very nice." She held up the black t-shirt with a purple Pink Floyd emblem on it. "All right, then, I'll make you a potion. It'll take me a while. You may as well come inside and wait."

Alyssa bent down to whisper in Max's ear. "Stupid dog, I'm out an MP3 player 'cause'a you." He ignored her and they followed Giserella into the cottage. The top of the doorway grazed Alyssa's hair and the ceiling inside wasn't much higher. When Giserella pointed to a wooden rocking chair in front of the fireplace, Alyssa sat in it.

Giserella bustled about, throwing things into an iron pot hanging from a metal hook that swung out from the fireplace.

Alyssa couldn't identify everything that went into the pot, but she saw a copper coin, several black feathers, a small block of wood, a handful of pebbles, an apple core, a dead rat, and a live snake. *This is so stupid.*

Giserella left the cottage and came back with a bucket that she emptied into the pot. She counted out seventeen drops from a blue glass bottle in the shape of a unicorn; the liquid emerged from its horn. She pushed the kettle over the fire.

Alyssa gripped the arms of the chair so she wouldn't bolt out the door, and stared at the pot. Finally, after what seemed like forever, she saw the liquid inside bubbling. Giserella dragged a tall stool over to the corner, climbed on it, and pulled a spiderweb from the ceiling. Holding two of the corners, she kept it intact until she draped it over the pot.

Geez, how disgusting is that?

Wiping her hands on her pinafore, Giserella sat in a smaller version of the rocker that held Alyssa. "How long has your grandmother had cancer?"

"Not quite a year." Alyssa swallowed her anger about the MP3 player and tried to be civil. "Mom says she might not make it 'til Christmas."

"Shoulda come sooner. She'll have to drink a lot. Make her take a glassful while standing on one foot and holding her breath every time she takes a piss 'til it's gone."

Alyssa stared. "Don't think Grandma can stand, never mind on one foot."

"Someone can support her, that's okay. But she's gotta hold her breath." Giserella rocked back and forth, kicking the floor with her heels.

Alyssa scrabbled about in her backpack until she found a scrap of paper and the dragon pen. She repeated the instructions as she wrote them down. "Glassful every time she pees while standing on one foot and holding her breath." She looked up. "She supposed to do all this while taking a leak?"

"No, she can do it after."

"Which foot?" *Does any of this matter. No way is this stuff going to work and Grandma shouldn't have to drink something so nasty.*

"Don't matter."

"How big a glass."

"Any size, just make sure it's completely full and she drinks it all."

Alyssa looked up. "So a shot glass and a water glass work the same?"

Giserella nodded. "Shot glass'll just take her longer to finish the jug, but if she's having trouble swallowing..."

Alyssa rolled back her eyes, but wrote that down too. Grandma was a stickler for precise instructions so she would bring her precise instructions. She tucked the paper into her pocket and returned the pen to her pack.

The snake in the pot screamed.

Giserella jumped up, pulled the snake out of the pot, and swung the kettle from the fire. Using a wooden ladle, she transferred the liquid in the pot to a purple clay jug bigger than Alyssa's backpack. Then she blew through the hole three times, and stuck a cork in it. "There ya go. Careful going back to the coach stop."

"Thanks a lot." If the stuff in the jug didn't work, no way would her dad buy her a new MP3 player. "I hope you like the music I have on the MP3 player."

"Music? No, I don't need any music, thanks."

Alyssa put on her backpack and struggled to hoist the jug up so she could carry it out of the cottage. "Stupid dog," she said as soon as the door closed behind them. "She doesn't even know what to do with my MP3 player."

"You're the one who decided to use your ticket to get a cure for your grandmother." Max trotted toward the path. "Not my fault you brought stuff you couldn't live without." He turned and looked over his shoulder. "Only two kinds of people visit Giserella: those who bring her presents that she likes and those she eats for supper."

Alyssa shuddered, and dismissed the idea as folderol, another one of Dad's favorite words. When she got to the path that led back to the road, she set the jug down. She couldn't carry it in her arms all the way back to the coach stop. After she stared at it for a few minutes, she pulled Max's leash from her pack, strung it through the two handles of the jug, and attached the clip to the loop. She lifted the leash onto her shoulder, resting it on the padded strap of her pack, and set off to follow the path back toward the road.

"Wrong way." Max headed in the other direction.

"But that's the way we came." Alyssa looked around, confused. She couldn't see Giserella's cottage.

"That's the way here; it's not the way back." Max kept walking.

"Now, hang on a minute. That just doesn't make sense. Why can't we retrace our steps?"

"Because this is Faerie, love," the mouse said. "The way in isn't the same as the way out."

Alyssa muttered under her breath. *And, I'm supposed to believe a stupid white mouse and a dog who gives away my stuff.* But she trudged off in Max's trail. The dog slowed until she caught up with him, and then resumed a brisker pace.

"Max, I've got to carry this pack and the jug. Don't go so fast."

"At this rate, it's gonna take us a couple of days to get to the coach stop." But he slowed his pace a little.

"How come we can't make it back to the

coach stop in a couple of hours? Only took us that long to reach Giserella's."

Max ignored her.

Stupid, stupid, stupid. Struggling to keep up with Max, Alyssa didn't have enough breath to rant out loud.

As they walked, the path became a road and the forest drifted into meadows. The meadows slowly became tilled fields of tall pink grass on one side and some kind of orange, bean-like crop on the other. Off in the distance, Alyssa occasionally saw an odd-shaped house or barn. One, although freshly painted, had such strange construction it looked like it would keel over at any minute. A little later, they passed a shed near the road with one wall and its roof missing. Odd shaped pieces of wood, rusted tools, and other debris littered the ground around it.

Alyssa had walked several yards past the mess when she stopped, turned around and walked back. She set down the jug and pulled a couple of round pieces from the pile of wood. *Wheels.*

Max sat down in the road.

Miss Lisle wiggled her whiskers. "What in the world are you up to?"

"If I have to traipse around Faerie for another day or two, I'm not lugging this jug." Alyssa dug through the pile and found two long poles, a shorter one, and a few square flat pieces with holes in them. "My shoulder's killing me already." She stripped off her pack and set the mouse on top of the jug.

She mucked around in the mess until she found a hunk of metal big enough to use as a hammer and a couple of dozen nails in various sizes and stages of rusting. *Good thing Mom talked Dad into letting me take woodshop.* One after another she held pieces together and pounded in nail after nail. She put the shorter pole through holes in the side pieces and attached that to the wheels. In the end, her contraption didn't look half bad. "Max, will you pull the jug for Grandma?"

He tilted his head to one side. "I suppose. Your grandma always gives me a big rawhide bone for Christmas." He licked his chops.

With him standing between the longer poles and the mouse making useless suggestions, Alyssa played with the leash until she came up with a way to attach it around the dog's chest, and leave enough slack to fasten it to the poles. She lifted the jug up into the makeshift cart. *Well that will give my shoulder a break, at least.*

She bent down and rubbed at the red marks in between her big and second toes. *This sucks. Shoulda changed into my sneakers when I found out how much walking I'm expected to do.* She yanked her socks and sneakers from her pack. After a moment's consideration, she took out her jeans as well. She just couldn't bring herself to wear Converse sneakers with a skirt. After she put the jeans on under her skirt and tied her sneakers, she stuffed the flip flops in the pack and hoisted it onto her back.

"You may as well put the pack in there, too. I don't think I'll notice the difference." Max stepped forward and the cart lurched after him.

Alyssa wedged her pack between the jug and the side of the cart. Without the heavy items slowing her down, she kept up a brisk pace. Even so, although the sun still blazed in a pristine blue sky, she needed to dig her hoodie out of the pack and pull it over her head. She noticed patches of ice in the fields on either side and, as the shadows grew longer, snow covered portions of the road and mud mucked up the rest of it. *Why me? How do I end up somewhere that it snows in the middle of August?*

She finally took pity on the shivering mouse and stuffed her into the fleece pocket across her belly. Only Max didn't seem concerned about the weather, although the mud and snow made it difficult for him to pull the cart.

"I thought Faerie would be more fun, romantic even." Alyssa pulled the hood over her head. "I mean where's Prince Charming? And, I haven't seen a single fairy."

Lilse stuck her head out of one side of Alyssa's pocket. "You didn't ask for a ticket to visit Prince Charming, love. You asked for a ticket to see Giserella."

"You mean, if I'd told the ticket lady I wanted to meet Prince Charming, I could be lolling around in some castle right now instead of trudging about through the snow?" *Why the hell didn't I think of that earlier?*

"Well, yes, love, although Prince Charming isn't one to allow visitors to loll about."

"And, you wouldn't have the magic to help your grandmother." Max wagged his tail.

Assuming the vile concoction Giserella poured into that jug actually works.

"Well, I suppose if I have to choose between meeting Prince Charming and helping Grandma..." *C'mon, no way Prince Charming'd have any interest in me anyway.*

Max yelped and Alyssa rushed to his side. He lifted his left front paw and she saw blood dripping from it. A large metal shard protruded from the pad.

This is so totally lame. What else will I have to put up with? Aloud, she said: "Poor baby, let me get that out of there." Blood gushed when she pulled the metal out. She grabbed his paw in one hand and squeezed, while reaching for her pack with the other. When she got the zipper open, she dug around until she found her cotton bikini briefs. She wrapped them around Max's paw, tying the pink fabric over the top.

Geez, now I'm using my underwear to bandage my dog. I should have stayed home. "Can you walk?"

"Not if I have to pull the cart."

Alyssa unfastened the cart poles from Max's harness and he limped off on three paws. She stood between the poles, lifted them, and followed. Despite the mud, pulling the cart beat lugging the heavy jug on her shoulder. Of course, she could just abandon it and concentrate on finding her way home. For all she knew that wicked little Giserella had filled the jug with icky stuff that wouldn't do anything to help Grandma. But, Alyssa had given up her MP3 player and the Pink Floyd t-shirt Dad had given her, plus an opportunity to meet Prince Charming and see real fairies. At least if she brought home something that helped Grandma, Dad might buy her a new MP3 player and let her get her belly button pierced.

"Max, do you know how much farther?"

"How much farther tonight, or until we get to the coach stop?"

Alyssa sighed. "Tonight, I guess." She didn't want to know how much longer she would be stuck here.

"Well, I don't think we'll find an inn on this road. We'll have to look for some kind of shelter."

Alyssa shivered. When the sun set, even if she huddled with Max all night, she didn't think she could survive in this cold. A tear crept down her cheek. *I think I liked it better when Grandma's presents didn't work.* She wondered how Max knew not only which road to take, but whether or not they would find a place to stay along the way.

The sun hovered at the horizon and Alyssa couldn't see well in the gathering gloom. But she glimpsed a dark spot in the hill above the road and hoped it was the entrance to a cave.

She couldn't pull the cart up the rough incline, so she tugged it off the road and behind a shrub, hoping it would stay put overnight. She put on her pack, used the leash to shoulder the jug, and struggled up the hill. The indentation in the hillside hardly qualified as a cave, but it would give them protection from the wind and the overhang would keep off any snow or rain.

Max ran off. Alyssa tucked the pack and the jug into a corner and gathered as many sticks, bits of dried bark, and the largest pieces of wood she could drag back to the shelter. Remembering Dad's instructions when he took her camping earlier in the summer, she piled the smaller sticks close to the outer edge of the shelter and stuffed some dried leaves underneath and in between. With the dragon pen/lighter, she lit the leaves, and when the sticks caught fire, she pulled one of the larger pieces of wood up against the flames. At least they could stay warm if she didn't let the fire go out.

Lilse crawled out of Alyssa's pocket and curled up in front of the fire. "Just lovely."

Alyssa ate two of the energy bars, and let the mouse have the crumbs in the wrappings. She worried about what she could feed Max. She didn't need to hear him whining that he was starving.

When he finally returned, Max had blood on his muzzle. Alyssa didn't want to think about what he had eaten. She poured small amounts of the bottled water into her hand and let him and Lilse lap it up. "One of us needs to stay awake and keep watch." That's what they did in every adventure story she had ever read and, if this wasn't an adventure, Alyssa didn't know what was.

Max sat down next to the fire. "I'll watch out while you get some sleep. I can roust Lilse when I need a nap."

Alyssa pulled two more big logs into the flames, curled up in front of the fire and, despite the hard ground, fell asleep in an instant.

Lilse woke her by pulling on her ear in the dark of night. "I need to sleep a bit more, love. Can you stand watch 'til dawn?"

Alyssa stretched her arms and sat up with her legs crossed in front of her. The fire had died down to embers. She rolled another log over the hot coals and watched until it caught. When she felt her eyelids grow heavy, she stood up and stepped out of the shelter far enough so she could look up at the black night sky, sprinkled with stars like powdered sugar on the French toast Dad burned when Mom let him make breakfast. She sniveled.

Max lay curled up with his tail over his nose and Lilse had settled into the crevasse between his haunch and his side.

Yesterday Alyssa had set off with no expectation that magic could work. She had forgone whatever pleasant adventures Faerie offered to bring home a huge, heavy jug because someone who allegedly ate people claimed it contained enough magic to save Grandma's life. Although she'd traveled a few hours to request the magic, so far her return trip had taken the better part of an afternoon and evening. Animals talked to her and kept watch and some even wore clothing. But other than that and some bizarre colors, Faerie didn't feel that much different from the rest of the world. *And, where are the damn fairies anyway?* She crept over to her pack and found her cell phone. She turned it on, and shut it off again when it failed to find a signal. *Figures.*

A screech sounded in the distance. When the sound got closer, she crawled back into the shelter. *Okay, I'm standing watch. What the bleep am I supposed do if someone or something actually tries to attack me?* Something howled in answer to the screeching. Next she heard a distant noise that sounded like a herd of elephants tromping through the woods. She jumped up and kicked dirt onto the fire until the glowing embers disappeared. If someone or something was stalking her, the fire would make her easier to find.

Alyssa huddled, shivering, against the back wall of the shelter until dawn tinged the edge of the sky with orange and pink. When the screeches and howls finally gave way to bird songs, Max sprang to his feet. Somehow, Lilse managed to stay on his back. With a sigh of relief, Alyssa stuck another energy bar in her pocket, shouldered her pack, and lugged the jug down to where she had left the cart. She hoped they wouldn't need to spend another night outdoors. For that matter, she really didn't want to spend another night in Faerie.

The cart sat where Alyssa had left it, but the wheels had disappeared. She sat down in front of it with her head in her hands and wept. *All that time building the stupid thing and now someone's taken it apart. I can't possibly carry this horrid jug around all day again.* Max rested his muzzle on his paws until she took a deep breath and stood up again. Crying wouldn't bring the wheels back. She put on her pack, slung the leash attached to the jug over her shoulder, and trudged down the road.

"Wrong way." Max turned in the other direction.

"But that's going back where we came from." Alyssa suppressed another sob.

"Yesterday it's where we came from, today it's where we're going." Lilse sat on Max's back, near his tail, clutching his fur in her paws. "Cheer up, love, if we make it past the gatekeeper, we should get to the coach stop by noon."

"Gatekeeper?" When the animals didn't answer, Alyssa turned and followed Max. Although he still limped, he did put some weight on his injured paw. At least Mom wouldn't yell at her for hurting her dog.

By the time she finished nibbling on the energy bar, they had reached a crossroad she hadn't seen the day before. A rocky path led off to one to side, into a dense woods where all the foliage was aquamarine.

Max looked back. "Watch me carefully. Only

step on the rocks that I do. The others aren't real."

Lisle had crawled up to Max's head and whispered in his ear. He jumped to a flat stone and reached his front paws out to another. Alyssa put one foot on the first rock and, when Max moved forward, her other foot on the second. Rock by rock, they worked their way through the trees. The jug weighed on Alyssa's shoulder. The air became oppressively hot. She wanted to take off her hoodie, but none of the rocks had room for her to set down the pack and the jug. She found it difficult to concentrate on which stones Max had stepped on.

"Watch it, love!" Lilse shouted.

Alyssa paused with her foot in the air poised to step on the next rock. Confused, she pulled her foot back and the stone disappeared into the muck.

"That one, to your left." The mouse pointed with one paw, while holding onto Max's ear with the other.

Alyssa stepped where instructed and tried to stay more alert. But the heavy air made her drowsy. Sweat trickled down her back and between her breasts and dampened the sweatshirt under her pits. *Great, as if I didn't stink bad enough.* She saw several spots off the path that looked inviting and safe where she could curl up and take a nap.

"Don't give up now, love," the mouse called. "We're so close. Honest."

After pulling her hoodie up from the waist over her chest, Alyssa switched the jug to her other shoulder and followed Max from stone to stone. With a final leap, he left the rocks behind and sat in front of a stone arch spanning the path. As soon as Alyssa's feet touched the dirt of the road, a giant with mottled red and blue skin emerged from under the arch. He stood even taller than her dad and his arms were the size of small trees. Bushy blue eyebrows stretched above red eyes that glowered at her. "Watcha want?"

Alyssa swallowed. At least he hadn't tried to eat her. "You must be the gatekeeper, sir. We're looking for the coach stop."

The giant growled. He looked at Max. "You look familiar. Been here before?"

Max stood up on his hind legs and pointed one paw toward Alyssa. "Yes, I visited here once with her grandmother. I believe the bear was white."

"Correct." The giant shook Max's paw. "You may pass."

Max dropped to all fours and went through the arch, but when Alyssa tried to follow, the giant put an arm across the opening. "Not so fast, Missy. You need to answer a question first."

"The bear was white?"

"Wrong answer."

"But you told Max it was correct." Alyssa set the jug down and removed the pack so she could pull her hoodie up over her head.

"Correct answer to the question I asked him." The giant moved so he stood in front of Alyssa. "You have to answer a different question."

Alyssa stuffed her hoodie back in the pack. "What question do I have to answer?"

"Justin left the Prince's castle the day before yesterday. He rode to the inn on the mountain which took him all day. He spent the night and rode to the cottage in the forest which took another day. Justin stayed overnight at the cottage and rode back to the Prince's castle in the morning. He arrived on Same Day. How is that possible?"

Alyssa stared at the giant. "How would I know?"

"That's your question." He sat down, legs crossed. "You don't get through until you answer it."

"Max!" Alyssa hollered, but the dog didn't respond and she couldn't see him.

Even sitting, the giant's head was at Alyssa's eye level. He looked like he could toss her over the arch if he chose.

"Ummm, how many tries do I get?"

"Just one."

"What if I answer wrong?"

"You can never leave Faerie." The giant leaned against one side of the arch and propped his feet up on the other. He wore green fringed moccasins that looked big enough for Max to crawl inside of and take a nap.

Alyssa put her head in her hands and wept.

Her dog and the mouse had deserted her and she had no idea how to survive in Faerie on her own. She had no clue how to answer the giant's question, and Grandma would die if she didn't. Plus, she'd never get to see Mom and Dad and all her friends or even, apparently, Max again.

"Please, Mr. Giant. I'm so very tired and I just want to go home. I'm only sixteen. I don't know anything about magic. I miss my mom. My grandma's sick. Can't you just let me go through?" She dug into her pack and pulled out her Swiss Army knife. "Can I use this to pay the toll?"

The giant grabbed the knife, and turned it over and over in his hands. "Thanks. But you still have to answer the question." He stuck the knife in the pocket of his green leather jerkin.

Alyssa hiccupped. Tears hadn't worked. Apparently, nothing in her pack would get her through the arch. She sat down and leaned her head against the jug.

"Umm, could you repeat the question?"

"Nope." The giant scratched his blue and red belly where it protruded below the belt that held his jerkin closed.

Alyssa thought about the riddle. She couldn't remember where Justin went, only that he rode about for three days and ended up getting home on the same day. Something about the puzzle struck her as familiar. She tried to remember the silly riddles her best friend Tory always repeated including the one that asked what color the bear was. She took a deep breath. "Justin rode a horse named Same Day."

The giant scrunched up his nose and made a noise in his throat that sounded like a fog horn. He stood up and stretched, stomped his feet, and stood to one side.

At first, Alyssa was too scared to move. Then she grabbed the pack and the jug and scooted through the arch, afraid he might change his mind. She saw Max sitting next to the road and heard the thunder of galloping hoofs in the distance. Shouldering the pack, she ran her fingers through her hair and resettled her hat with the brim to one side. Of course, after two days of mucking about Faerie without a bath, she most likely looked frightful. *My face is probably covered in zits.*

Four black geldings pulled a striped red and blue coach to a stop in front of her. A large tabby cat in pink livery stepped down. "Ticket, please." The cat purred.

Alyssa plucked the mouse from Max's head and held her up for the cat to see. It opened the coach door.

"We part ways here, love." Lilse crawled up Alyssa's arm to her shoulder. "This coach'll take you home and you've no further need for a ticket." She gave Alyssa a peck on the cheek. "Hope what's in the jug does the trick for your gram."

"Thanks for your help." Alyssa lifted the mouse from her shoulder and set her on the road.

"My pleasure, love. Cheerio." The mouse scampered back toward the arch.

Alyssa set the jug on the coach floor, pushed it toward the other side, and hauled herself up into the empty carriage. Max jumped up behind her. She took off her pack, braced herself in one corner of the front-facing seat, and fell asleep.

The next thing she knew the cat was calling to her through the open door of the coach. "This is your stop, Miss."

She dragged the jug and her pack out of the coach, set them down on the bench inside the bus stop shelter, and watched the coach disappear around a bend in the asphalt highway. When she dug her cell phone out of her pack and turned it on, it got a signal right away. She leaned her back against the shelter wall and slid down to the seat, tears of relief leaking out of her eyes. She dialed her home number. Fortunately, her mom answered.

"Mom, it's Alyssa. Can you come pick me up at the school bus stop down by the highway? I'm just too tired to drag this jug up to the house."

"What jug? Never mind." Her mother sighed. "I'm sorry you couldn't make the magic work this time either, dear."

"But, I did, Mom. It wasn't much fun, actually it was pretty nasty, and I had to give up my MP3 player to get a magic potion for Grandma. That's what's in the jug. Magic from Faerie."

"How in the world? You only left the house

an hour or so ago." Her mother paused. "How long were you in Faerie, Alyssa?"

"Two horribly long days." Alyssa blinked back tears. *I shouldn't cry now, I'm almost home.*

Mom gasped. "I'll drive right down to get you."

Alyssa ended the call. At least Mom would believe her. She knew Dad wouldn't and didn't plan to tell him, even if that meant he wouldn't let her get her belly button pierced or buy her a new MP3 player. *My friends'll think I'm nuts if I try to explain where I went.*

Max rested his head on her lap and she scratched his ear. "Must be hard not being able to talk." He just looked at her with big brown eyes and wagged his tail. She patted the jug. "At least we got this boy. At least we got this."

If the magic worked, she promised herself, she would spend the two weeks before school started with Grandma. Maybe she would let Alyssa try again on some of the presents from before. *I still have a lot of freckles, and this year the jazz band's supposed to go to New York City.*